ELLA

Diaries

TOP SECRET!

Meredith Costain

With special thanks to the Year 5 & 6 students
from Gold St PS and Boroondara Park PS—M.C.

For my School Camp buddies Bridget,
Andrea, Nicole, Rachel and Claudia—D.M.

Danielle McDonald

First American Edition 2018
Kane Miller, A Division of EDC Publishing

Text copyright © Meredith Costain, 2016
Illustrations copyright © Danielle McDonald, 2016

First published by Scholastic Australia, a division of Scholastic Australia Pty Limited in
2016. This edition published under license from Scholastic Australia Pty Limited.

Library of Congress Control Number: 2018932772

Printed and bound in the United States of America

2 3 4 5 6 7 8 9 10

ISBN: 978-1-61067-837-7

ELLA
Diaries

WORST CAMP
EVER

Kane Miller
A DIVISION OF EDC PUBLISHING

Monday evening, in my top bunk, just before lights-out

Dear Diary,

Our class is at camp! For a whole week! yay!!

The camp is called Camp Courage and it is right in the middle of the bush. The bus took SIX WHOLE HOURS to get here. And I didn't get bus sick. Not even once! Even on the bendy, windy road parts through the mountainous mountains.

Mountainous Mountains

Raf did though. Eww. I'm glad I wasn't
sitting next to *him*.

Camp Courage is aMAZing.

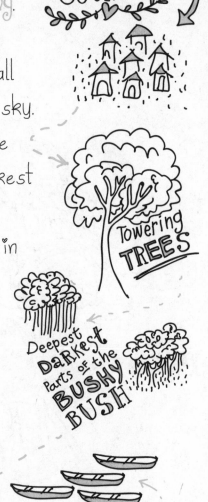

There are towering trees all
around us, as high as the sky.
And hiking trails that take
you into the deepest, darkest
parts of the bushy bush.
And a gigantic lake right in
the middle, with sweet
little boats for two that
live at the side of it.

GIGANTIC LAKE

SWEET LITTLE BOATS

✳ 6 ✳

This is the third time I've been to a school camp. I LOVE them! They are always fabulously FABulous!

THINGS I LOVE about {SCHOOL} CAMPS

① Being in The Great Outdoors. You can do excellent outdoorsy stuff like boating and swimming and hiking and discovering exotic new plants.

IN DOORS

OUT DOORS

2 Seeing lots of interesting and unusual animals you never see at home.

Koala

GOANNA

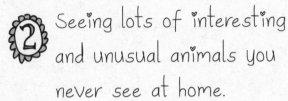
Wedge-Tailed EAGLE

special NEW kind of Praying MANTIS

3 Playing pranks on your fellow campers.

RUBBER SNAKE
sleeping BAG

AAARRRRRGH!

4 Telling spooky stories around the campfire at night.

There's only one teeny tiny problem about school camps.

It is EXTREMELY hard to find a secret, safe hiding place to keep secret things—like YOU, Diary—safe from PRYING EYES.*

* Prying eyes are what people who are always trying to sniff out your private, personal, confidential, classified secrets have. (They probably have PRYING NOSES as well.) Prying eyes look like this:

PRYING EYES

TOP SECRET
DO NOT LOOK
INSIDE

So I made a cunning TOP SECRET secret disguise for you to wear while you're at camp with me.

WHAT unusual ANIMAL IS THAT? A FIELD GUIDE AND WORKBOOK

(FAKE) DUST JACKET

MY DIARY

EVERYONE at this camp knows how much I LOVE drawing and writing and talking about interesting and unusual animals. So now I can pretend to be writing FACT FILES about all the animals I find here, when ~~acksh~~ actually I'm writing in you, Diary!

YESSSSSSSSSSSS! I also made extra sure
I got one of the top bunks in our cabin by
putting my

BOOK-
BAG

BACKPACK

Sleeping
BAG

PAJAMA
CASE

Toiletry
BAG

Extra pillow
in case the
camp PILLOW
is LUMPY

(To remind ME of BOB
waiting LOYALLY
at HOME)

on the bed as soon as we came in the door.
That way it will be harder for any prying-
eye people to see what I'm doing. Which is
just as well. Because guess what?

Peach Parker—the person with the biggest prying eyes in the history of people with prying eyes—is IN MY CABIN!

Bleuchhh!

Peach

And so are her two annoying friends, Prinny and Jade.

Prinny

JADE

NOOOOOOOOOOOO!

It's SOOO not fair, Diary. Why couldn't the teachers put nice, friendly NON-prying people in my cabin? Like Chloe. Or Georgia. Or Poppy.

~~Forch~~ Fortunately Zoe (my BFF) and Cordelia (who happily is a NON-pryer) are in my cabin too. And darling Mr. Wombat, who goes EVERYWHERE with Cordelia. Because if I had to share a cabin with Peach all by myself for even five minutes, I would DIE.

But just to make sure (in case sharing with Peach became too much for us and we ALL died) I asked Mr. Appleby✶✶ if Zoe, Cordelia and I could please change to a DIFFERENT cabin.

✳✳ Mr. Appleby is in charge of the whole camp. He makes all the important decisions like who gets to go in which cabin, and what types of jam we get to put on our toast at breakfast.

But he just gave me a big frowny frown that made his eyebrows wriggle around like wiggly caterpillars and said, "No changes allowed. Under ANY circumstances. Even unforeseen ones," and walked away.

caterpillar EYEBROWS!

MR. APPLEBY

So now we're stuck in a tiny cabin in the middle of the bush with Princess Peach and her yucky friends. For a WHOLE WEEK.

Ms. Weiss just came in to tell us it is lights-out in ten minutes and if we aren't all tucked up in our sleeping bags like bugs in a rug when she comes back around there is going to be BUG BIG TROUBLE.

And we'd all have to peel potatoes for the
camp kitchen for the rest of the week.

BLEUCHHH!

I HATE peeling vegetables of ANY kind.

I haven't brushed my teeth or washed my
face yet, so I'm going to stop writing now,
Diary, even though there is heaps more to
tell you about what happened today.

Bye!
Sweet dreams.
Ella
XOXO

Tuesday morning, very, very early

Dear Diary,

I am writing this from my top bunk where I am curled up like a baby echidna inside the top part of my sleeping bag.

I am all curled up because I can't stretch my legs out in case my feet parts touch THE THING in the bottom part of my sleeping bag.

ME

THE THING

Top part OF my SLEEPING BAG

?!!

I am not even 100% sure what THE THING is. But it is exTREMEly squishy.

I know this because last night when I climbed into my sleeping bag, the very tip of my toe touched it. I was too scared to pull out THE THING so I could see it properly in case it was something REALLY gross. Or stinky. Or disGUSTing.

my toe

Something SQuiSHY

And I couldn't scream like a BIG BABY (even though I wanted to) because then the person who put it in there would know their prank had worked.

NO SCREAMING!

Bleuchhh. NO WAY was THAT going to happen.

So I just slept all night with my legs pulled up instead. Ha!

I bet Peach put THE THING in there. I am SO going to get her back. (He-he.)

Everyone else is still asleep and SNORING like gigantic steam trains. So I will tell you some more about what happened yesterday.

First of all, the camp leaders, Mr. Appleby and Ms. Da Gama, divided us all up into four mixed teams. The teams are named after really cool animals.

TEAM NAMES:

Possums

Stingrays

Barracudas

Bandicoots

Our team is the Barracudas✳, which is the best name for a team in the history of team names!

✳ Barracudas are long, skinny, gigantic fish that can swim really fast. They look quite sweet until they open their jaws and show you their ferocious fangs teeth. I wish I could have a pet one. I would call him Barry.

Barracuda
with mouth CLOSED

Barracuda
ferocious TEETH
with mouth OPEN

WHO is in the {Barracudas}

1 Everyone in our cabin (including our mascot, Mr. Wombat).

MR. WÖMBAT

2 Peter and Raf and the other boys in their cabin—George, Billy, Zac and Tariq.

Peter   Raf   George   Billy   ZAC   TARIQ

(STINKY BOYS. Bleuchhh!)

We have to do EVERYTHING together, like kayaking, and damper making and going on Night Walks in the bush. If your team does really well, you earn points. But if anyone on your team does something silly, like messing around when you're supposed to be listening, you LOSE points! That is SO not fair. ☹

At the end of camp, the team that gets the most points wins a trophy.

YESSS! The mighty Barracudas are going to win that trophy for sure!

Our first activity was kayaking.✳✳

✳✳ A kayak is a looooooong thin boat for one or two people that is exTREMEly hard to stand up in without tipping it over. In fact, I think they should change its name to a tipit.

KAYAK

Another interesting fact about kayaks (and tipits) is that the word is exactly the same if you run around to the other side of it and read it backward. See?

KAYAK = KAYAK

You say it like this: KY-YAK. Though I am not 100% sure why its name has a yak in it because there were no yaks in any of our boats or even tied up by the side of the lake. I checked.

KY-

We all had to put on our bathing suits and life jackets and sun hats and sunscreen and meet Mr. Appleby at the lake. Here is a picture of me in my super-stylish water-sports outfit that I spent ALL last week throwing together (stylishly).

STRAW-fringed HAT

COOL Sunscreen PATTERNS

Sparkly BEADS with stylish TEARDROP Pendant

BLINGED-UP BACKPACK

JEWEL-ENCRUSTED ☆ Flip-flops

Glitterized SARONG

Zoe and I were together in the same boat.
And guess what our boat was called?

The *Titanic*!

The *Titanic* is the ~~worserest~~ worst name for
a boat in the history of boat names! That's
because once upon a time a famous ship
called the *Titanic* bumped into a gigantic
iceberg and sank down

        down

        down

          to the very

            bottom of

              the sea.

~~Forch~~ Fortunately there are no icebergs in our lake. ☺

~~Unforch~~ Unfortunately our boat was very tippy! ☹

watery water started splashing up over the top part. And the bottom part got wetter and wetter.

And so did the bottom part of our feet.
And then the top part of our feet.
And then our knee parts.
And then our boat started sinking!

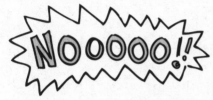

Mr. Appleby started WAVING FURIOUSLY
and yelling out from the shore.

So we tried to climb out of our kayak and into the one next to it.

And guess who was in that one?

Peach Parker. And her precious friend Prinny. They pushed our kayak away with their long stick things so we couldn't get in their boat.

Peach and Prinny are SOOOOO MEAN!!!

Then Georgia and Chloe used THEIR long stick things to bring their boat over next to ours. So we climbed into that one instead. ~~unforch~~ Unfortunately I slipped a bit on the way in.

And guess what happened next? You never will so I'll just tell you.

Peach and Prinny laughed at me. Like this:

And they were so busy laughing they forgot
to watch where they were going.

Their boat crashed into Peter and Raf's boat.
And Peach and Prinny
fell into the water and
got all wet. And then Mr.
Appleby jumped into the
water to save them.

MR. Appleby

And then Peter and Raf jumped in too.
(Only they didn't try to save Peach and Prinny.
They just swam around a lot, having fun.)

And so did all the rest of the Barracudas.
Including me and Zoe!

Peach and Prinny were bobbing around on the top of the water screaming "HELP! HELP!" just like BIG BABIES. The water wasn't even THAT DEEP.

And Peter and Raf started pretending to be REAL barracudas, with snapping jaws and gigantic teeth. They swam around in circles going "SNAP! SNAP!" at Peach and Prinny and all the NON-real Barracudas.

And then all the NON-real Barracudas
(including me and Zoe, but NOT Peach and
Prinny) joined in and started swimming
around going "SNAP! SNAP!" back at them.
And then we all had a

BiG WATER Fight!

It was FUN! And EXcellent! And fabulously
FABulous!

I don't think Peach
and Prinny thought so

Peach

Grrrrrr!

though. Princess Peach HATES getting her
precious hair wet. ☺☺

Mr. Appleby made us all stop being REAL
barracudas and swim back to shore
like boring, plain old people instead of
MONSTERS OF THE DEEP.

And then he deducted ten points from our
team for being noisy. Which
is so not fair. It wasn't
OUR fault Prinny and
Peach laughed at me.

MR. APPLEBY

And if they hadn't laughed at me, they wouldn't have crashed into Peter and Raf's boat. Or fallen in.

And if Peach and Prinny hadn't fallen in, Peter and Raf and all of the rest of the Barracudas wouldn't have jumped in after Mr. Appleby, and swum around noisily pretending to be REAL barracudas with snapping jaws.

So it's ALL their FAULT!

TEAM: BARRACUDAS	
POINTS WON	POINTS LOST
	Kayaking -10

I have to stop writing now, Diary! Everyone
is starting to wake up.

CU soon.

E x

PS Oooooo. I almost forgot. Last night, I think
I heard a yowly howling sound, coming
from the deepest, darkest part of
the bush. I wonder what it was?

yowling.
HOWLING

Tuesday morning, just after breakfast

Peach just found a squashed fake spider with fake blood dripping off its fangs in the bottom of her sleeping bag and screamed like a big baby AGAIN.

I have absoLUTEly NO IDEA how it got in there (he-he).

ARRRRGHHH!

squashed
(FAKE) SPIDER

Peach

Tuesday, after lunch

Dear Diary,

This morning we did more team activities. First we played a game of volleyball against the Bandicoots.

Volleyball

And we won! So our team gets twenty points toward the Grand Trophy.

YESSSSSSS!!

TEAM: BARRACUDAS			
POINTS WON		**POINTS LOST**	
Volleyball	20	Kayaking	-10

After volleyball, Mr. Appleby told all the
Barracudas to line up near the flying fox.
Which is just WEIRD because everyone
knows that flying foxes ONLY COME
OUT AT NIGHT, and it was
eleven o'clock in the morning!

I was just starting to tell him this when Peach put up her hand like she does at school and called out over the top of me in her really whiny, icky teacher's pet voice: "Oh, I just LOVE going on a flying fox, Mr. Appleby. I went on one SIX TIMES last Christmas when we were on vacation in Timbuctoo."

Precious
Peach - - - →

Mr. Appleby gave her a big smile and asked what her name was. It's SO unfair, because if she hadn't butted in, he would have been asking me for MY name for knowing interesting facts about unusual animals like flying foxes.

And then Peach gave him a big smile back and said, "Peach Parker" and Mr. Appleby made this really bad Dad Joke about both of them having "fruity" names.

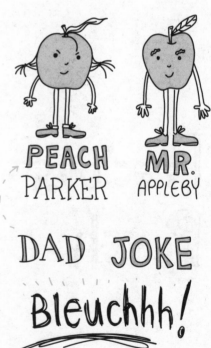

PEACH PARKER   MR. APPLEBY

DAD JOKE
Bleuchhh!

And then he said, "OK then, Peach Parker. You can go first and show everyone else what to do."

And then Peach turned around and gave me a big sneery smirk. And I gave her an even BIGGER
sneery smirk back. Flying foxes are really, really small. No way was Peach EVER going to fit on a flying fox, even if Mr. Appleby found one out here in the bush and woke it up.

I was just whispering all this to Zoe and telling her what a big fake Peach was, when Zoe whispered something back. Something HORRIFICALLY HORRIFYING.

Mr. Appleby was talking about a DIFFERENT kind of flying fox. Zoe told me there are actually TWO kinds.

Ooops. Just as well I didn't say anything to Peach.

Kinds of FLYING FOXES

1 The one that eats flowers and fruit and is a type of bat.

SLEEPS in THE DAYTIME

FOLDED WINGS that STRETCH OUT like an UMBRELLA WHEN it's FLYING

Hangs UPSIDE DOWN from BRANCHES

FACE LIKE A FOX'S FACE

2 The one made of poles and wires that sends you whizzing through the treetops. A zip line.

TREETOPS

Wires

POLES

Whizzing KIDS

And we were all going to go on the
SECOND kind of one.

So then we all stood in a line while Peach
climbed up a tall ladder to the very top
part of a high platform and Mr. Appleby
connected her up to some ropes and
belt bits. And then all of a sudden she
WHIZZED OFF to the other side of the
campground.

While she was whizzing she did all of these
FANCY PANTS flips and moves like she
always does in gymnastics class. And everyone
clapped and went WOO HOO!

EsPECially the boys.
Peach is just a
BIG SHOW-OFF.

Then Prinny had a turn.
And Jade.

And Raf.

And then it was MY turn next.

And then butterflies started FLUTTERING
around inside my stomach.

And whirlpools started WHIRLING around
in my ears.

And my brain went all FIZZY, like it was going to explode into a gazillion trillion pieces.

Whirling WHIRLPOOLS

EXPLODING BRAIN

FLuttering BUTTERFLIES

So I swapped places in the line with Zoe. And then with Cordelia. And then with all the other Barracudas who hadn't had a turn yet.

And then I was the last person in the line
and there was no one else left to swap
with.

So I ran back here to the cabin and hid
until it was time for lunch. ☹

Tuesday, about five minutes later

Dear Diary,

You're probably wondering why I ran away when it was my turn to go on the flying fox zip line. I'm just as good as Peach at doing flips and fancy moves because of all the gymnastics and ballet stuff I do, so it should have been easy-peasy for me.

BUT it's <u>NOT.</u>

It's because

Sorry, have to go now,
Diary. Ms. Weiss just
came in to do a cabin
check and reminded me
it's time for Afternoon
Activities. And I don't
want to lose points for our team by being
late. I'd be in SO MUCH TROUBLE with
the other Barracudas if *that* happened.

E

Tuesday, after dinner

Dear Diary,

Guess what we had for dinner tonight!

And schnitzel with canned peas and corn and mashed potatoes and extra gravy!

All of my most favorite things. I ate some of EVERYTHING.

Zoe found a hair in her
mashed potatoes. Eww. It was
long and woolly. Maybe it was
from one of the yaks?

This afternoon all the groups did a team
challenge, called Hut Building. There were two
main important rules.

HUT-BuiLDiNG RULES:

1 Your hut has to be big enough for the
WHOLE TEAM to fit inside.

2 Make sure the sides of your hut don't
leak so you won't get wet if it rains.

The kind teachers gave us some very helpful big poles to start us off. But then we had to find everything else ourselves out in the wild wilderness, just like the pioneers* did.

* Pioneers were brave people who built sweet little houses in places with no roads or Internet or fences to keep out the fierce wild animals that also lived there.

Pioneer

So we all went tramping off into the bush like ~~ragged~~ rugged explorers from the olden days.

This is what our team found.

THING that was FOUND	WHO found it	USEFUL or **NOT** ✓ = USEFUL ✗ = NOT USEFUL
LONG knobbly **FALLEN** Branches	ZOE and **ME**	✓ ✓ ✓
STRIPS of BARK	CORDELia	✓ ✓ ✓
(NOTHING)	Peach	✗ ✗ ✗ ✗ ✗⊕ SHE didn't want TO **GET** her PRECIOUS PRINCESSY hands DIRTY

Zoe and I were GOBSMACKED** when Peter and Raf came back with poop.

** Gobsmacked is a word Nanna Kate uses. It means you are amazed and astonished and shocked to the power of 900 trillion.

This is what we said.

Me (holding my nose): Kangaroo poop? Eww.
Zoe (also holding her nose): That is disGUSTing.

Raf (rolling his eyes): Come o-o-o-o-n. Kangaroo poop is PERFECT for hut building.

Peter: Yeah. You can squish it up with your fingers and fill in all the cracks with it.

Raf: Yeah. You heard what the teachers said. No leaks.

Me (sighing): There aren't going to BE any cracks OR leaks. Because Zoe's and my sticks and Cordelia's pieces of bark are EXACTLY the right size and shape and will fit together PERFECTLY.

Zoe: Yeah. Just like a gigantic jigsaw puzzle.

Me: So THERE!

Zoe: Yeah. Who needs your gross old kangaroo poop anyway?

Raf: Fine, build it yourself then.
Peter: Yeah. Good luck.
George: See ya.

And then Raf and Peter and George and all the rest of the boys walked away and took turns doing skids on the rusty bike and having ~~competishuns~~ competitions to see who could flick the most pieces of kangaroo poop into a bucket WITH THEIR FINGERS.

Bleuchhh. Boys should just be BANNED from camps altogether.

Have to go now, Diary. We're all going on a
Night walk. In the dark! with flashlights!
It is going to be FABulous!

Yours forever,
Ella xoxo

PS Our team didn't win the Hut-Building
competition. The Stingrays did. ☹☹☹

TEAM: BARRACUDAS

POINTS WON		POINTS LOST	
Volleyball	20	Kayaking	-10
Flying Fox	20		
Hut Building	0		

And guess what? The teachers tricked us!
It wasn't raining, but they tested our huts
by throwing gigantic buckets of water over
them! While we were all inside! That is SO
MEAN!

It was exCEPtionally funny though.
EsPECially when Princess Peach's precious
hair got wet. AGAIN (he-he).

THE BARRACUDAS' HUT

THE STINGRAYS' HUT (Bleuchhh!!)

The Stingrays' hut was the only one that didn't leak. And guess what they used to fill in the cracks in the walls? ☹☹

Tuesday night, about five minutes later

I just went to get my warm jacket out of my bag for the Night walk and it wasn't there! And neither was Zoe's!

And in the place where our jackets were supposed to be were BOYS' UNDIES!!!

And I actually touched them. And now I have BOY GERMS all over my hands.

Ewww.

Tuesday night, about ten minutes after that

We finally found our jackets. They were in the boys' bathroom.

Double EWWWW!!

Peach is <u>so</u> going to GET iT.

05

Tuesday night, late, on my bunk

Dear Diary,

The Night walk was aMAzing!

All the teams got to go on different trails, like the horseback-riding trail or the lake trail. The mighty Barracudas went on the scariest one—deep into the deepest, darkest, creepiest part of the bush. It was so EXCITING!

First of all we did a STAR Search.

The sky was very black and dark. We could see lots of different stars and shapes. Ms. Weiss and Ms. Da Gama told us some of their names. Like:

THE MILKY WAY

And

THE SOUTHERN CROSS

And there was a scorpion!

And a giant eagle!

(SCORPIUS)

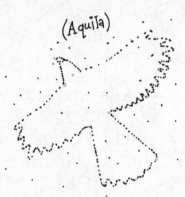

(Aquila)

Then Ms. Da Gama told us to find our OWN shapes. And I saw a unicorn!

Well, it LOOKED like a unicorn.

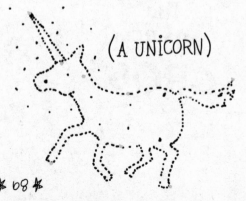

(A UNICORN)

And then after that, we all sat down in a big circle and George told us a SPOOKY STORY his brother Harry heard when HE was here at camp. It was all about a man called Fred who used to come camping here with his cat Tilly. In EXACTLY the same place as us.

Which is just WEIRD. Who ever heard of a camping cat?

FRED'S tent

Tilly's TENT

Tilly

FRED

BUSH RAT

TILLY

And then one day Tilly ran off into the bushes after a ratty bush rat! And Fred ran off after her. And while Fred was running he slipped on some mossy rocks and hit his head and his brains came out. Then he died a sad and tragic death. And now he is a GHOST!

FRED THE GHOST

And then George said that every year, on the sad anniversary of his tragic death, the ghost of Fred comes back to the campsite, looking for Tilly.

And guess when the anniversary is?

TODAY!!!

Then Billy joined in and told us we had
to be EXTRA careful where we stepped.
Because Fred's ghost might be out walking
too, and we might step on his toes!

And then Peter and Raf started making
SCARY GHOST NOISES, like this:

WOOOOOOOO!!!

RAAAAARRRR!!!

And then Prinny started
blubbing like a BIG BABY
and saying NO WAY was
she going walking in the
dark if there were ghosts out there.

Prinny

And then Ms. Weiss tried to calm her down
by saying it was just the boys being silly.

And Cordelia patted her arm and said, "Don't
worry, Prinny. Ghosts aren't even REAL."

So then Prinny stopped blubbing and we all set off very slowly and carefully, being exTREMEly careful about where we put our feet (just in case ghosts actually ARE real). Princess Peach and Prinny and Jade went first, because they always have to be THE FIRST and THE BEST at EVERYTHING.

As we walked we listened to the windy wind sighing through the trees

and the frogs croaking

CROAK!

and the lizards rustling

and the koalas grunting

GRUNT!

and the night birds hooting.

HOOT!

And then all of a suddenly a "thing" with a glowing face jumped out of the bushes right in front of us and went "BOOOO!"

And then another one jumped out right behind us and went "BOOOO!"

And we all crashed into each other.

And Peach started screaming "GHOST! GHOST!" and running around like a maniac.

And so did Prinny and Jade.

And so did everyone else in our group (including me and Zoe).

The Good News

It wasn't ghosts. It was Peter and Raf,
messing around with their flashlights. This
is how they did it.

STEP 1

Pull your sweater
up over the back
of your head.

STEP 2

Shine a flashlight
under your chin bit
so people can't see
your face bits.

The Better News

Peter and Raf got into trouble for being silly and frightening the animals that live in the bush. And Ms. Da Gama marched them back to the campsite and made them peel potatoes. (Ha!)

The Bad News

When Mr. Appleby found out what they did on the Night walk he deducted ANOTHER ten points from the Barracudas. All these points we keep losing are making my head spin!

+20 -10 0 +10 -10

After Peter and Raf had left, everyone else kept going on the Night walk. This time there were no ghosts with glowing bits or boys jumping out of the bushes going "BOO!"

We all just walked along REALLY quietly,
looking and listening. Even Peach was quiet.

We saw a baby possum and its
mom in a tree!

And a tawny frogmouth!

And the moon playing
hide-and-seek with us between
the trees!

It was aMAZing!

So amazing I wrote this poem.

Possum

BABY

TAWNY
FROGMOUTH

MOON

TREES

Night walk

The bush after dark
Is different from daytime
All the night animals
Come out for playtime!
Scuttling lizards
And frogmouths in trees
Upside-down possums
Swing on a trapeze.
Witchy-hand branches
And silvery moon
I hope we can go on
Another walk soon!

Have to go now, Diary. Ms. Weiss just came around to tell us it was time for lights-out.

Sweet dreams.
Love,
Ella xxx

Tuesday night, about five minutes later

The lights are back on again.

Mainly because Prinny looked out the window as she was climbing into her bunk and saw all of Jade's and Peach's and her

undies hanging off
the big bush right
next to the flagpole.

He-he-he. I wonder
how they got there?
☺

Tuesday night, about twenty minutes after that, by flashlight

You'll NEVER guess what just happened!

Everyone was in bed in the dark and
Cordelia was telling us all a spooky story

about six girls in a cabin at a camp just like this one. And in the story they were all getting ready to go to bed when there was a knock on the door. And then one of them goes over to open the door and . . .

Da-da-da . . . DUMMMM.

There's nobody there.

And then just at that very exact same moment . . .

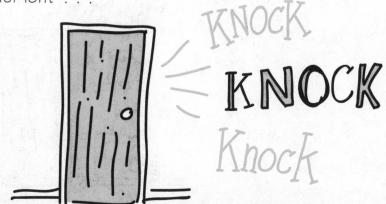

KNOCK
KNOCK
Knock

There WAS a knock on the door.

OUR DOOR!!!

And everyone started screaming like BABIES! (Except me and Zoe. Well, maybe just a little bit.) Again!

I immediately went into ninja attack mode and stealthily climbed down from my bunk to find out who was at the door before Mr. Appleby heard all the screams and deducted even MORE points from our team.

ME (NINJA ATTACK MODE)

I was silently crouching in ninja-crouch stance, getting ready to open the door, when Zoe called out, "Don't open it, Ella! What if it's the ghost of Fred, come to haunt us forevermore?"

And everyone started screaming again.

And then Cordelia whispered, "Take Mr. Wombat with you. He's very brave."

MR. WOMBAT

So I stealthily crept ninja style over to Cordelia's bunk and picked up Mr. Wombat (and also a gigantic flyswatter in case the door knocker WAS a ghost and I needed to swat it).

THEN I stealthily crept
back over to the door
and opened it.

And there was
nobody there.

AAARRRRGGHHHH!!!

Peach JADE Prinny ME ZOE CORDELIA MR. WOMBAT

Wednesday morning, before breakfast

This is what Zoe and I looked like when we woke up this morning.

And Mr. Wombat was halfway up the flagpole.

xxx.

Wednesday morning, straight after breakfast

Dear Diary,

Guess what?!

Something very exciting and important happened at breakfast this morning.

Zoe and I were telling Georgia and Chloe and Poppy about how the boys got into trouble for making ghost noises last night on our Night walk. And they said that the Possums (that's the name of their team) heard noises when they were out on *their* Night walk too!

Except their noises weren't fake, phony ones, like ours. They sounded like this:

RRROOOOOWWWWRRR!!

And then we all had a BIG THINK about what might have been doing the RROOOWWWRRRing.

Here are our guesses:

1 A WEREWOLF

2 TWO WEREWOLVES

That was it. Nobody had any other ideas.

And then Zoe said it couldn't have been a werewolf, or even *two* werewolves, because anyone with even a tiny brain knows that werewolves aren't ~~acksh~~ actually real. They are just made-up creatures you see in scary books and movies.

And then Chloe said, "Are you sure?"

And Zoe said, "One hundred percent. I did a project on them once."

And then Poppy started jiggling around in her chair like a teabag being jiggled in a cup of tea, and said, "Ooooooooo!"

Poppy

Oooooooo!

And everyone said, "What?!"

And Poppy said, "Maybe it was the black panther!!!"

And everyone said, "WHAT black panther???"

And then Poppy looked at us with shiny eyes and told us all about how her cousin Lily came here for HER school camp last month.

SHiny
EYES

And Lily and her friends heard lots of RROOOWWWRRRing sounds when they went on their Night walk too.

And this other girl told them about a big black panther that escaped from a traveling circus about 900 years ago and now lives up in the hills. And every now and then it leaves its ~~liar~~ lair✳ and comes down to the campsite and howls, late at night.

HOOoWL!

* A lair is what you call a place where a wild animal—like a bear or a tiger or a wolf—lives. A liar is someone who makes up stories that aren't true, even a teeny tiny bit.

So now we have to look out for the black panther AND the ghost of Fred.

It's all getting very confusing!

Have to go now, Diary. We all need to tidy up our cabin in case Ms. Weiss does a spot inspection and we lose even MORE points.

CYA!
Love, Ella

SPOT inSPECTiON!

Ms. Weiss

Wednesday, while everyone else is at lunch ☹

ME

desperate
DESPAIR

Dear Diary,

I am in desperate despair.
So desperate I will probably have to borrow
one of the ~~tipits~~ kayaks and row it out
into the middle of the lake so I don't ever
have to talk to anyone EVER AGAIN. Ever.

Especially girls with fruity names that
rhyme with blood-sucking
creatures that grab on to
your ankle when you're
out walking in the bush.

BLOOD-SUCKING
LEECH

BUSHWALKER

ANKLE

Here's what happened after breakfast.

We were all rushing around the cabin doing tidying-up stuff like sweeping (me and Cordelia) and picking up clothes from the floor (Peach and her buddies) and taking the trash can to the trash room to empty it (Zoe).

And while I was sweeping I was happily singing this sweet little song I made up, called "Black Panther in the Night."

It goes like this.

Black panther
Black panther
Black panther in the night.
Black panther
Black panther
Gives campers a big fright.
Aaaarrro-o-o-o-o-o-o-o-o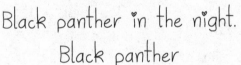
 Aaaarrro-o-o-o-o-o-o-o-o
Black panther in the night.

And then Zoe came back from the trash room and told me something Horrifically Horrible. So Horrifically Horrible I'm not sure I'll be able to write it down without getting you all wet.

Here's what we said:

Zoe: We're doing team activities again this morning. And guess what our team is going to be doing?
Me: Designing our costumes and tiaras for when we go up on stage to collect the Grand Trophy at the end of camp?
Zoe: Nope. Guess again.

Me: Making musical
instruments out of twigs and
forest grasses so our team
can play them while I sing my
aMAZing and FABulous new
song "Black Panther in the Night"?
Zoe: Nope. Guess again.
Me: Taking Peach and her
annoying friends way, way
out into the middle of the
bush and leaving them there
to find their way home again?
Zoe: Nope. Guess again.
Me: I give up. What are we doing?

And then Zoe spoke the Words of Doom.

We were going on the Giant Swing.

AAAARRRGGGHHH!

The Giant Swing is the most scary, terrifying, petrifying thing in the history of scary, terrifying, petrifying things. On a scale of 1 to 10 it is 1,000,000,000,000 to the power of 100,000,000,000, which is a number so big nobody has ever been able to write it down.

SCARY

Terrifying

Petrifying

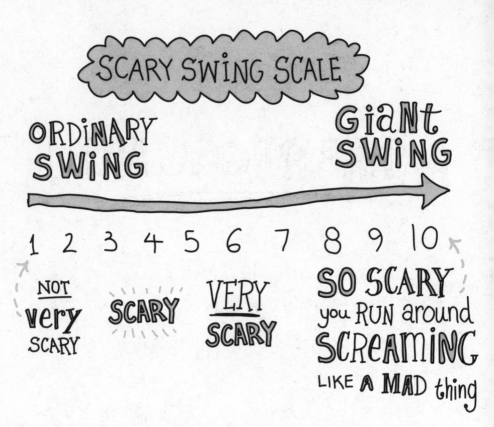

SCARY SWING SCALE

ORDINARY SWING → GIANT SWING

1 2 3 4 5 6 7 8 9 10

NOT **very** SCARY   SCARY   **VERY** SCARY   SO SCARY you RUN around SCREAMING LIKE A MAD thing

It is especially scary for people who are scared of being up high. Like me. ☹

Which is just WEIRD because hardly ANYTHING scares me.

THINGS I AM <u>NOT</u> SCARED OF

SPIDERS

GHOSTS

THUNDERSTORMS

FEROCIOUS BARKING DOGS

Being **SUCKED** down the Drain iN The BATHTUB

PEACH PARKER (m<u>ost</u> of the time)

THINGS I AM SCARED OF

 HiGH PLACES

 SURPRISE MATH TEST

DOING a **SURPRISE** MATH TEST WHILE i'm iN **HiGH PLACES** LiKE THE TOP OF a

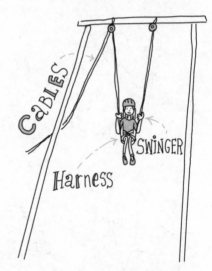

CABLES

SWINGER

Harness

GiANT SWING

It took a LOOOONG time for us to get to the Giant Swing place. This is because I kept thinking of reasons why I had to go back to our cabin.

REASONS WHY I HAD TO GO BACK TO OUR CABIN

1. I needed to change into my lucky socks.

LUCKY
SOCKS

2. I needed to get a tissue in case being on the Giant Swing gave me a nosebleed.

TISSUES

3. I needed to get ANOTHER tissue, in case the first one broke from all the blood.

When we finally arrived, we lined up with all the other Barracudas. Mr. Appleby asked who wanted to go first.

And guess who did?  Princess PEACH (OF COURSE)

Mr. Appleby strapped her into the harness bit. And then all of our team pulled on a long rope and Peach went straight up into the air,

and HIGHER . . .

and HIGHER

HIGHER

until she was at the very top part of the Giant Swing.

And then all of a sudden she started swinging from side to side, like this:

PEACH

And then Prinny had a turn, and Jade and George and Raf and Cordelia, with Mr. Wombat strapped to her back.

CORDELIA

MR. WOMBAT

And everyone else in the Barracudas, until there was no one left and it was MY turn.

I was just about to say, "I'm SOOO sorry, Mr. Appleby, but I can't go on the Giant Swing right now because I need to go back to camp and make an emergency phone call," when Zoe tugged my arm and whispered, "You can do it, Ell. You can do ANYthing."

So I took a deep breath and
I turned to Mr. Appleby and said,
"Bring it on!" instead.

Mr. Appleby gave me a big, cheery smile
and helped me put the harness bit on.
And all the rest of the team pulled on the
rope. And I went

                        and HIGHER . . .
            and HIGHER
    HIGHER
and then my tummy went all wobbly and
my brains started fizzing around inside my
head. I called out:

until they stopped pulling the rope, and I came straight back down to the nice, flat, NON-high ground again. **PheWWW!!**

Peach gave me one of her smirky smirks. Then she turned to Mr. Appleby and said, in her whiniest, ickiest,

SMIRKY SMIRK

teacher's pet voice, "Can I have another turn, please, sir? The Giant Swing is the BEST THING EVER. When I grow up I want to be a Camp Leader just like you."

BLeuchhh!

And guess what? Mr. Appleby awarded our team an extra ten points for Extreme Enthusiasm By a Member.

GRRRRR!

Sometimes Peach makes me so mad I want to THROW UP!!!

TEAM: BARRACUDAS

POINTS WON		POINTS LOST	
Volleyball	20	Kayaking	-10
Flying Fox	20	Night Walk	-10
Hut Building	0		
Extreme Enthusiasm	10		

Wednesday night, very, very late

Dear Diary,

Something really, really SCARY happened tonight. SO SCARY everyone is shaking in their ~~boots~~ bunks, too afraid to go to sleep.

Here's what happened.

Scene: In our bunks, just after lights-out.
Peach (annoyingly): I just LOVE going on the Flying Fox and the Giant Swing. It's SO fun. I hope we get to do it again tomorrow. Don't you, Ella?

Don't you, ELLA?

Me: (Silence)

Peach (even more annoyingly): Oh, that's right. I forgot. You can't go on things like that because you are a scaredy-pants BIG BABY.

Prinny: Shhhhhhh.

Peach: What do you mean, "Shhhhhhhh"? Don't "Shhhhhhh" me. How rude!

Prinny

Shhhhh

Prinny: I mean, shhhhhhh, listen! There's . . . something outside our cabin.

Zoe (rolling her eyes): Yeah. Like trees.

Me (also rolling my eyes): And other cabins.

Jade: Shhhhhhh!!! I just heard it too!

Zoe: Heard what?

Jade: A kind of . . . huffing, puffing, snuffling sound.

Heard
What?

zoe

Like a . . . MONSTER that can't
BREATHE properly!

Prinny: Or a . . . a ghost
with a cold!

A GHOST with a COLD!

Peach: Or a . . . a black panther!

Or a... black PANTHER!

Zoe: Well, I can't hear it.

Me: Same. Can you hear it, Cordelia?

Cordelia: Nope. And neither can Mr.
Wombat.

peach

Peach: AAARRRGGGHH!

Zoe: What???!!!

Peach: Footsteps! Loud
ones! Outside our cabin!

Footsteps! LOUD ONES! OUTSIDE OUR CABIN!

Jade: And more puffing!

Scary Thing Outside:

PEACH

SCRATCH! SCRATCH! SCRATCH!

Everyone in the cabin:

Thursday morning, before breakfast

Dear Diary,

Just letting you know that we are all still alive. In case you were wondering.

Love, Ella

Thursday, just before lunch

Dear Diary-doo,

Something fabulously fabulous happened this morning!

We were doing another team challenge. This time it was a cook-off between the Mighty Barracudas and the Powerful Possums!

Ms. Weiss gave us all mixing bowls and spoons and

FLOUR WATER

AND SALT

and showed us how to make damper* over a campfire.

* Damper is a yummy type of fake bread that you make when you are in the middle of the bush and there are no stores nearby to buy REAL bread. It is ALWAYS black and burnt on the outside and gooey and raw in the middle.

Black and BURNT

Gooey on THE iNSiDE

LOAF OF DAMPER

Then the boys on our team decided it would be A GOOD IDEA to roll up their damper mix into squishy little balls and flick them at the girls. And Zoe and I thought it would be an even BETTER IDEA to flick our damper mix back at them. (Especially when some accidentally on purpose landed in Peach's hair.)

And then everyone in the Barracudas started yelling, "Food fight! Food fight!" and throwing bits of THEIR damper around. And then we started flicking bits of damper at the Possums. And the Possums started flicking bits back.

Mr. Appleby's eyebrows went all wriggly
again. Then he deducted ten points from
BOTH teams for playing with our food.

TEAM: BARRACUDAS

POINTS WON		POINTS LOST	
Volleyball	20	Kayaking	-10
Flying Fox	20	Night walk	-10
Hut Building	0	Damper Making	-10
Extreme			
Enthusiasm	10		

Then Ms. Weiss and Mr. Appleby showed us all how to poke a pointy stick through the bits of damper we had left and wave it over the hot coals until it cooked. And yummy cooking smells wafted all over the campsite.

yummy COOKING SMELLS

WAFT WAFT

HOT COALS

I was just pushing a
pointy stick through my
uncooked damper when I

HUFF
PUFF

ME

heard the huffing, puffing sound again. And
then another sound like Bob makes when he's
sitting under our table hoping you'll pass him
down bits of food you don't want to eat, like
broccoli. And peas. And ~~collyflower~~ cauliflower.

And then Prinny pointed into the bushes and
said, "Look! It's the black panther!!"

And then she screamed, like this:

AAAARRRGGGHHHH!!!

PRINNY

And so did Jade. And then guess who
screamed the loudest?

And guess what else?

The scary thing in the bushes wasn't even a
black panther. It was a BIG, black, hungry cat!

And it looked EXACTLY like Nanna Kate's
cat, Smiggen. (Except for the black bits. And
its being gigantic.)

---MEDIUM-sized
tabby

GiGaNtic bLacK cat

Cats are my third favorite animal (after praying mantises and dogs). I am NEVER, EVER scared of them, even if they are big and ~~furrocious~~ ferocious with giant claws and lashing tails and sharp, pointy teeth.

So I decided to play a BIG TRICK on everyone (especially Peach). He-he. Here's what I did.

First of all I had a quick Top Secret Emergency Meeting with Zoe.

Zoe listened to my exciting Plan. And then she said,

ELLA, you are BRILLIANT!

And I said, "I KNOW!"

It was SO EXCITING!

Then Zoe and I did a little play in front of
everyone, while they looked on admiringly,
impressed by my courage and bravery.
Here's what we said.

Me (bravely): I've made up
my mind. I'm going to stop
that black panther
in its tracks, right now.
Zoe (dramatically): No,
Ella, you can't!
Me: But I fear I must.

Zoe (anxiously): But . . . but what if the black panther snatches you up in its big, sharp teeth and rips you up into teeny, tiny pieces?

Me: Then so be it. But I must protect the rest of the campers AT ALL COSTS! Even if it means (pause for small sob) risking my own life.

Zoe: You are a true BFF—and ~~saver~~ savior of all.

Me: I know.

Then I immediately went into ninja-mission mode, and craftily crept toward the camp table that had all our bits of damper on it.

I checked to see that everyone (especially Peach and Mr. Appleby) was watching. Then I quietly took an already-cooked damper off the table, and cleverly crept toward the big, black cat, lurking hungrily in the bushes.

I waved the damper at the cat so I could lure her out of the bushes with its yummy smell, then carefully threw it down on the ground in front of her.

ME

LURE
(DAMPER)

I waited until the big cat was ripping up my lure into teeny, tiny pieces with her ferocious, vicious, pointy teeth. Then I stealthily removed my belt (it was my second-best stylish pink one with the braided bits on the sides Nanna Kate gave me for Christmas) and popped it around her gigantic neck. I did the buckle up so she couldn't escape and hung onto her by the end bit.

MY (second-BEST) BeLT

Damper

THE BiG CAT

Next, I sent a series of complicated hand signals to Zoe to tell her to announce that I had heroically conquered "the beast."

Zoe sent me a series of complicated hand signals back to say that she would.

Then I casually strolled back to the damper-making area, leading my conquered beast on her (super) stylish pink leash.

Everyone said really cool things, like:

(Except Peach, who just stood there glaring at me with a scowly scowl on her face.)

Mr. Appleby took the cat and said he would call the Lost Animals Home to see if anyone had lost their pet. Then he gave the Barracudas an extra ten points for Courage in the Face of Danger.

ZOW-EE!

TEAM: BARRACUDAS

POINTS WON

Volleyball	20
Flying Fox	20
Hut Building	0
Extreme Enthusiasm	10
Courage in the Face of Danger	10

POINTS LOST

Kayaking	-10
Night Walk	-10
Damper Making	-10

Thursday, after lunch

Dear Diary,

Everyone (except Peach) was talking about me at lunch. They said I was a HEROIC HERO and a STAR!

Brave? Me? I can't even go on the Flying
Fox or the Giant Swing without my stomach
wobbling and my brains fizzing over. ☹☹☹

And then I had a **BRilLiant IDEA!**

But a little bit scary too . . .
Have to go now, Diary.

CUL8R,
E

Thursday night, in my bunk, very, very late

Dearest, darlingest Diary,

The rest of today was excellently excellent.

We had more of my favorite things for dinner.

And then all the teachers dressed up in funny outfits and sang silly songs.

And then we watched a movie Ms. Da Gama made about some of the funny things we did while at camp.

But the BEST THING was that I went on the Flying Fox.

ME!!!

SCAREDY-pants ELLA!

It was the Possums turn to go on it. So I asked Mr. Appleby if I could join them, just for today. And he said yes! ☺

Mr. Appleby put the harness bits on me. I closed my eyes.

Then I opened them again.

Then I closed them again.

ME!

Flying
FOX

Then Mr. Appleby pulled the rope bit and I went whizzing off through the trees like a gigantic bird.

WWWHHHEEEEEE!

It felt like I was FLYING!

And then I got to the end and I opened my eyes and it was all over.

And guess what I said? You never will so I'll just tell you.

Good night, Diary.
Sweet dreams.
Love, Ella xx

Friday, on the bus home

Dear Diary,

That was the
BEST CAMP EVER!!

After breakfast, we packed everything up and cleaned out our cabins. Then everyone had to go back to the dining room so Mr. Appleby could present the awards.

MR. APPLEBY

The Bad News
We didn't win the Grand Trophy.

BOO-hoo.

⚹ 137 ⚹

The Good News

The Possums did! Yay for Poppy and Chloe and Georgia! They beat the Stingrays by 10 points.

YAY!

🌿 FINAL RESULTS 🌿	
Possums	60
Stingrays	50
BARRACUDAS	30
Bandicoots	20

The Better, Fabulously Fabulous News
I won a special BRAVERY AWARD!

It was for going on the Flying Fox, even though just thinking about it almost made my head spin!

CAMP COURAGE
BRAVERY AWARD
Presented to
ELLA
for courage in facing her
fears on the FLYING FOX
☆ ☆ ☆ ☆

Everyone cheered and clapped when I went up to accept it. Especially Zoe.

Yours 4 EVER,
Ella

PS (five minutes later)

Oops—I forgot to tell you the most important thing!

Zoe and I finally got Peach back last night.

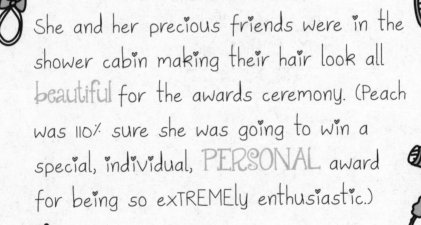

She and her precious friends were in the shower cabin making their hair look all beautiful for the awards ceremony. (Peach was 110% sure she was going to win a special, individual, PERSONAL award for being so exTREMEly enthusiastic.)

And then when she turned the hair dryer on, baby powder blew out of the blowy part. And it landed all over her hair and her face and her

Baby Powder!

HAIR Dryer

PEACH

clothes. And all over Prinny's and Jade's clothes. It took them so long to get it off they missed the start of the awards ceremony.

He-he-he. It's an old prank Nanna Kate told me she used to do when SHE was at camp, about 900 years ago.

PPS (Five days later)

Guess what? You know how Mr. Appleby called the Lost Animals Home about the big, black lost cat? Well, Ms. Weiss just told me they found her owners!

They live on a farm a long way away from Camp Courage. And one night there was a big, scary, thunderous thunderstorm and their pet cat ran away and got lost in the bush. They've been looking for her for weeks!

And guess what her name is?

Hmmm . . . I wonder . . .

Read more of Ella's brilliant diary